Dear Parents,

Congratulations! Your child has embarked on an exciting journey – they're learning to read! As a parent, you can be there to support and cheer them along as they take their first steps.

At school, children are taught how to decode words and arrange these building blocks of language into sentences and wonderful stories.

At home, parents play a vital part in reinforcing these new-found skills. You can help your child practise their reading by providing well-written, engaging stories, which you can enjoy together.

This series – **Ready, Steady, Read!** – offers exactly that, and more. These stories support inexperienced readers by:

- gradually introducing new vocabulary
- using repetition to consolidate learning
- gradually increasing sentence length and word count
- providing texts that boost a young reader's confidence.

As each book is completed, engaging activities encourage young readers to look back at the story, while a Picture Dictionary reinforces new vocabulary. Enjoyment is the key – and reading together can be great fun for both parent and child!

Prue Goodwin
Lecturer in Literature and Children's Books

520 496 40 2

How to use this series

The **Ready, Steady, Read!** series has 4 levels. The facing page shows what you can expect to find in the books at each level.

As your child's confidence grows, they can progress to books from the higher levels. These will keep them engaged and encourage new reading skills.

The levels are only meant as guides; together, you and your child can pick the book that will be just right.

Here are some handy tips for helping children who are ready for reading!

Give them choice – Letting children pick a book (from the level that's right for them) makes them feel involved.

Talk about it – Discussing the story and the pictures helps children engage with the book.

Read it again – Repetition of favourite stories reinforces learning.

Cheer them on! – Praise and encouragement builds a child's confidence and the belief in their growing ability.

KU-503-317

LEVEL 1 For first readers

* short, straightforward sentences
* basic, fun vocabulary
* simple, easy-to-follow stories of up to 100 words
* large print and easy-to-read design

LEVEL 2 For developing readers

* longer sentences
* simple vocabulary, introducing new words
* longer stories of up to 200 words
* bold design, to capture readers' interest

LEVEL 3 For more confident readers

* longer sentences with varied structure
* wider vocabulary
* high-interest stories of up to 300 words
* smaller print for experienced readers

LEVEL 4 For able readers

* longer sentences with complex structure
* rich, exciting vocabulary
* complex stories of up to 400 words
* emphasis on text more than illustrations

Make Reading Fun!

Once you have read the story, you will find some amazing activities at the back of the book! There are Excellent Exercises for you to complete, plus a super Picture Dictionary.

But first it is time for the story . . .

Ready?

Steady?

Let's read!

Elizabeth Baguley   Gregoire Mabire

MEGGIE MOON

LITTLE TIGER PRESS
London

Digger and Tiger
spent all their time in
the Yard. No one else
dared to come in.
It was *their* place.

Digger and Tiger were rough-and-tumble boys, spiky-haired, hole-at-the-knee boys. They were not brothers, but they went together like a dustbin and its lid.

One day a girl arrived.
She stared at the king-of-
the-castle boys. The boys
stared back.

"I'm Meggie Moon,"
said the girl. "Can I play
with you?"

"This is *our* yard,"
snarled Tiger.

"We don't want to play
with you," hissed Digger.

"Are you sure?" said
Meggie, laughing.

Meggie went off to explore.
She had ideas.

She picked up
some rubbish . . .

and began to arrange it . . .

until . . .

"It's a racing car!" said Tiger.

"You can drive it if you want,"
said Meggie.

"Not likely," said Digger.

But as soon as Meggie left, the boys jumped in the car and raced away until dark.

The next day, Digger
and Tiger watched
Meggie picking
through the junk.

"Build something!"
ordered Tiger.

So Meggie made
a ship and the boys
played pirates.

"Can I come
aboard?" she asked.

"I suppose so,"
said Tiger.

Meggie climbed to the top of the mast.

"Enemy ship ahoy!" called Meggie.

The boys were startled.

"Aye-aye, shipmate!" they said.

On the third day
Meggie said, "Why
don't we make a den?"

She found wall-things
and roof-things and
they all played there
until dark.

Every day, Meggie thought of something different.

"She's not bad – really," Digger admitted to Tiger.

Then one day Meggie announced,
"I'm going home tomorrow."
"But what shall we play when
you've gone?" wailed Digger.

"I've brought you a goodbye present,"
she said. "You can play with that."
And she toppled a tower of junk into
the yard.

"Star troops at the
ready!" she called
as she left.

"Aye-aye, Captain,"
Digger and Tiger saluted.

The boys looked at each other.
They had ideas.

"Star troops!" barked Digger.

"At the ready!" shouted Tiger.

By dusk, smooth things, shattered things and battered things spiralled high above the Yard fence.

The astronauts climbed into their rocket.
  "Blast off!" they cheered. And Digger
and Tiger shot off skywards in the
Starship Meggie Moon!

Excellent Exercises

Have you read the story? Well done!
Now it is time for more fun!

Here are some questions about the story. Ask an adult to listen to your answers, and help if you get stuck.

Great Games

This story is about three friends who love playing games. What games do *you* like to play?

Amazing Imagination

Can you name some of the objects in this picture? What would *you* make from a pile of old rubbish?

Super Ship

Now describe what Meggie Moon is doing in this picture.

Awesome Adventure

Can you remember what Digger and Tiger made at the end of the story? Where do you think they will go in it?

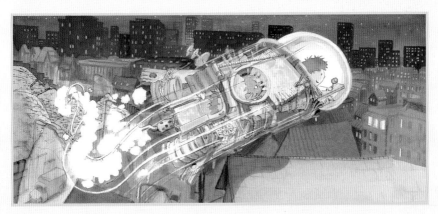

Picture Dictionary

Can you read all of these words from the story?

car

Digger

Meggie

pirates

rocket

rubbish

saluted

stared

Tiger

toppled

Can you think of any other words that describe these pictures – for example, what colours can you see? Why not try to spell some of these words? Ask an adult to help!

The Biggest Baddest Wolf

Harum Scarum is the biggest, baddest, hairiest, scariest wolf in the city. And he loves to frighten people! But when he loses his teddy, he doesn't seem so scary after all . . .

Mouse, Mole and the Falling Star

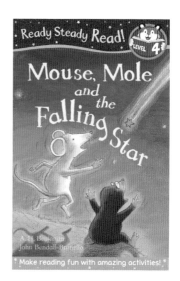

Mouse and Mole are the best of friends. They share everything. But when a shooting star zips across the sky, they both want it for themselves. Could this be the end of a beautiful friendship?

The Nutty Nut Chase

The animals are having a race! And the winner gets to eat a delicious, brown nut. But the race does not go as planned. And the nut seems to have a life of its own!

Robot Dog

Scrap the Robot Dog has a dent on his ear. So he is sent to the junkyard, with the other rejected toys. Will he ever find an owner?

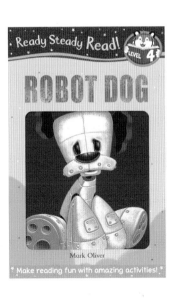

For Kate and Anna — E B
For Louise, from Greg!

LITTLE TIGER PRESS, 1 The Coda Centre, 189 Munster Road, London SW6 6AW
First published in Great Britain 2005
This edition published 2013
Text copyright © Elizabeth Baguley 2005, 2013
Illustrations copyright © Gregoire Mabire 2005, 2013
All rights reserved
Printed in China
978-1-84895-680-3
LTP/1800/0600/0413
2 4 6 8 10 9 7 5 3 1

Books in the Series

LEVEL 1 - For first readers

Can't You Sleep, Dotty?

Fred

My Turn!

Rosie's Special Surprise

What Bear Likes Best!

LEVEL 2 - For developing readers

Hopping Mad!

Newton

Ouch!

Where There's a Bear, There's Trouble!

The Wish Cat

LEVEL 3 - For more confident readers

Lazy Ozzie

Little Mouse and the Big Red Apple

Nobody Laughs at a Lion!

Ridiculous!

Who's Been Eating My Porridge?

LEVEL 4 - For able readers

The Biggest Baddest Wolf

Meggie Moon

Mouse, Mole and the Falling Star

The Nutty Nut Chase

Robot Dog